The USS Arizona Story

by Cynthia Kennedy Henzel

Content Consultant

William M. Fowler Jr.

Distinguished Professor Emeritus
Northeastern University

Famous *Ships*

Essential Library

An Imprint of Abdo Publishing | abdopublishing.com

abdopublishing.com

Published by Abdo Publishing, a division of ABDO, PO Box 398166, Minneapolis, Minnesota 55439. Copyright © 2018 by Abdo Consulting Group, Inc. International copyrights reserved in all countries. No part of this book may be reproduced in any form without written permission from the publisher. Essential Library™ is a trademark and logo of Abdo Publishing.

Printed in the United States of America, North Mankato, Minnesota
102017
012018

THIS BOOK CONTAINS
RECYCLED MATERIALS

Cover Photo: Department of the Navy/Bureau of Ships/National Archives and Records Administration
Interior Photos: Naval History and Heritage Command, 4–5, 11, 29, 43, 55; Department of the Navy/Office of the Chief of Naval Operations/Naval Observatory/National Archives and Records Administration, 7; Red Line Editorial, 13, 44; US Navy/Naval History and Heritage Command, 15, 61, 75; Library of Congress, 16–17; Courtesy of M. DeSomer/Naval History and Heritage Command, 18–19; Department of the Navy/Bureau of Yards and Docks/New York (Brooklyn) Navy Yard/National Archives and Records Administration, 23; Department of Defense/Department of the Navy/Bureau of Ships/National Archives and Records Administration, 24–25; USS Arizona Collection/AZ 517 Box 17 Folder 19/courtesy of University of Arizona Libraries, Special Collections, 30–31; USS Arizona Collection/AZ 517 Box 10 Folder 32/courtesy of University of Arizona Libraries, Special Collections, 33; USS Arizona Collection/AZ 517 Box 53 Folder 4/courtesy of University of Arizona Libraries, Special Collections, 34; USS Arizona Collection/AZ 517 Box 19 Folder 42/courtesy of University of Arizona Libraries, Special Collections, 38; US Navy/National Archives/Naval History and Heritage Command, 40–41, 48–49, 52–53, 57; Bettmann/Getty Images, 47; Boston University Medical Library and Archives/Navy Medicine, 59; Robert Kradin/AP Images, 64–65; AP Images, 67; Farm Security Administration/Office of War Information Black-and-White Negatives/Library of Congress, 69; Office for Emergency Management/War Production Board/National Archives and Records Administration, 72; Corbis Historical/Getty Images, 76–77; Mass Communication Specialists 3rd Class Diana Quinlan/US Navy/National Park Service, 79; Michael Ochs Archives/Getty Images, 81; Chris Curtis/Shutterstock Images, 82; Audrey McAvoy/AP Images, 85; iStockphoto, 86–87, 92; National Park Service, 89; Andrew Cooper/Getty Images Entertainment/Getty Images, 94

Editor: Kate Conley
Series Designer: Craig Hinton

Publisher's Cataloging-in-Publication Data

Names: Henzel, Cynthia Kennedy, author.
Title: The USS Arizona story / by Cynthia Kennedy Henzel.
Description: Minneapolis, Minnesota : Abdo Publishing, 2018. | Series: Famous ships | Includes online resources and index.
Identifiers: LCCN 2017946798 | ISBN 9781532113222 (lib.bdg.) | ISBN 9781532152108 (ebook)
Subjects: LCSH: USS Arizona Memorial (Hawaii)--Juvenile literature. | Arizona (Battleship)--Juvenile literature. | Hawaii--Juvenile literature.
Classification: DDC 940.5426--dc23
LC record available at https://lccn.loc.gov/2017946798

Contents

⚓ *The USS* Arizona *was a Pennsylvania-class battleship that was larger and better armed than previous navy vessels.*

Chapter 1

A DAY OF INFAMY

The wake-up call sounded in the still air at 5:30 on Sunday morning, December 7, 1941, and the crew members of the battleship USS *Arizona* tumbled from their hammocks. Spirits were high. After coming back from maneuvers on Friday, the battleship had taken on 1.5 million gallons (5.7 million L) of oil for a scheduled trip to the West Coast of the United States.[1] Pearl Harbor, Hawaii, was beautiful, but it was a long way from home, and the crew was looking forward to being reunited with family and friends.

The ship also carried 180,000 gallons (680,000 L) of aviation fuel for the scouting planes it carried and 1 million pounds (454,000 kg) of gunpowder.[2] The crew was prepared if an attack came at sea on the journey across the Pacific Ocean.

Out at Sea

At 5:50 a.m., as the USS *Arizona* crew prepared for the day, Japanese warships were approximately 220 miles (350 km) north of Oahu.[3] Admiral Isoroku Yamamoto, commander in chief of the Combined Fleet of Japan, had devised a plan to cripple the US armed forces, leaving Japan free to expand into the South Pacific. Six aircraft carriers plus destroyers, tankers, two battleships, and three submarines prepared to attack. The weather was less than favorable; the sea was choppy, and heavy clouds made for poor visibility.

At 6:10 a.m., the carriers turned into the wind for the airplanes to take off. A total of 183 bombers, fighters, and torpedo planes roared from the decks and joined in formation behind Commander Mitsuo Fuchida, leader of the attack that was headed for

Mitsuo Fuchida

After World War II (1939–1945), Mitsuo Fuchida cooperated with the Americans during interrogations and provided valuable information about the attack on Pearl Harbor. He became an author, writing books about the Japanese military experience during the war. After converting to Christianity, he toured the United States and other parts of the world as a missionary in the 1950s.

6

Mini-Bio ⚓

Isoroku **Yamamoto**

Commander in Chief
of the Combined Fleet of Japan

Admiral Isoroku Yamamoto (1884–1943), head of the Japanese navy, conceived and planned the attack on Pearl Harbor. He was a brilliant strategist and realized Japan could not hope to win a war with the United States unless its forces could first weaken the naval defenses in the Pacific. If a war went longer than a year, he told the Japanese prime minister, they did not have a chance of winning. The United States had vast natural resources and labor that could produce weapons if the nation needed to fight. Yamamoto's plan, a surprise attack using aircraft carriers to launch bombers, torpedo carriers, and fighter planes on Pearl Harbor, was a success, but he was not sure the victory would last. He wrote: "I fear all we have done is to awaken a sleeping giant and fill him with terrible resolve."[4] He was right. Seven months later, at the Battle of Midway, the tide of the war turned in the United States' favor. Admiral Yamamoto was killed in 1943 when his airplane was shot down by US forces.

Pearl Harbor.[5] Fuchida was an experienced bomber pilot who commanded all air groups of Japanese Carrier Division I.

On the USS Arizona

By 6:30 a.m., showered and shaved, the crew of the USS *Arizona* headed for breakfast. It was a leisurely breakfast of powdered eggs with ketchup, fried Spam—a canned meat—pancakes, and coffee. Many were dressed in casual clothes—pressed white shorts and white T-shirts—because it was a Sunday morning. Some men settled in to read the newspaper.

Likely, some discussed their time on liberty in Honolulu the day before. They had gone ashore to the restaurants, shops, and bars; toured the island; or enjoyed Waikiki Beach. Curfew was midnight for most, and 2:00 a.m. for officers. Others that morning may have rehashed the movie, *Dr. Jekyll and Mr. Hyde*, that played on the fantail the night before.

Beyond the USS Arizona

At 6:45 a.m., the US destroyer *Ward* sank a Japanese minisubmarine that was prowling too close to Pearl Harbor. It was just after 7:00 a.m., time for watch change at the Opana radar outpost. The two privates on duty noticed a group of 50 blips on the radar screen and reported this to Lieutenant Kermit Tyler at the Fort Shafter information center.[6]

Tyler, in only his second day on the job, remembered that he had been told to expect incoming American B-17 Flying Fortress Bombers and assumed that was what the radar station had picked up. For security reasons, he couldn't tell the radar operators the American airplanes were expected, so he told them, "Well, don't worry about it."[7] Shortly after, a second wave of airplanes took off from the Japanese aircraft carriers.

Decoding Warnings

At 7:15 a.m., the code clerks at army headquarters decoded the message from the USS *Ward* about the sunken submarine. They sent it to Admiral Edward Kimmel, commander in chief of the Pacific Fleet. The admiral read the message and decided to wait for verification before taking any action.

In Washington, DC, meanwhile, US code breakers intercepted a message that appeared ominous. The message from Tokyo, Japan, was sent to the Japanese

Radar

Radar works by sending out radio waves and detecting reflections of the waves from distant objects. Britain had developed a network of radar stations called Chain Home in the years before World War II to detect incoming German airplanes. But the new technology took time to implement, and the mobile station at Pearl Harbor had been running for less than 30 days. Radar became increasingly important during the war as it was deployed on ships to detect incoming attacks.

9

negotiators in Washington at 7:33 a.m. It ordered Japanese negotiators to break off talks with the United States.

Thinking this might mean war, General George C. Marshall, the army chief of staff, sent a message to Lieutenant General Walter C. Short, commander of US Army forces in Hawaii, to warn of the impending conflict. However, conditions in the atmosphere were poor for radio signals, and the message did not get through.

In the Air

At 7:40 a.m., as the Japanese airplanes approached Pearl Harbor, the clouds broke, and Fuchida saw the white sand coastline of Oahu. He sent out the order to attack: *to, to, to*. Then he sent a second message: *ra, ra, ra*. This message, interpreted by some as *tora, tora, tora*, told the Japanese carrier that the stealth attack was successful. The Americans had no idea the Japanese were coming.

At 7:55 a.m., Japanese aircraft struck the first US airstrip. The aircraft there were parked close together to make it easier to protect them against sabotage. But this only made them an easier target from the air. No one had expected an aerial attack.

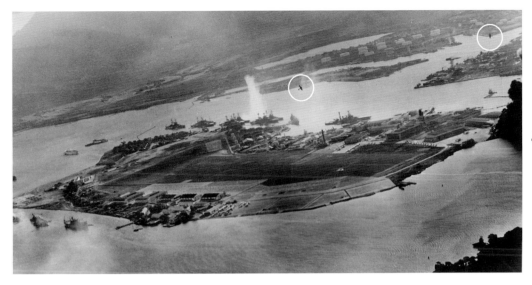

⚓ *A photograph taken from a Japanese plane amid the torpedo attack shows Japanese planes,* circled, *ready to bomb the Navy Yard over Ford Island.*

Torpedoes and B-17s

At 7:55 a.m., Lieutenant Commander Logan C. Ramsey looked out the window from inside the Ford Command Center. He spotted a low-flying airplane and assumed it was a careless US pilot. He looked more closely to see if he could identify the airplane so he could report the pilot.

As he looked up, Ramsey saw a long black object fall from the airplane: a torpedo! He immediately sent out a message to warn the fleet: "AIR RAID ON PEARL HARBOR X THIS IS NOT DRILL."[8]

Around this time, the expected B-17 Flying Fortress Bombers arrived at Oahu. To save weight on the long flight from the West Coast to Pearl Harbor, the aircraft were not armed. The pilots had expected only a stop in Oahu for refueling before continuing to the Philippines.

Unable to defend themselves or fight to defend Pearl Harbor, the B-17 pilots dodged Japanese aircraft.

Corporal E. C. Nightingale's Account

Marine Corporal E. C. Nightingale was on the USS *Arizona* as it was attacked. He later shared his story, explaining that during the attack he suddenly found himself in the water, swimming for his life. Approximately halfway to a pipeline, his strength gave out. There were other men in the water, and Major Alan Shapley, seeing Nightingale about to go under, grabbed his shirt and told him to hold on. Approximately 25 feet (7.6 m) from the pipeline, Shapley began to struggle to keep them afloat. Nightingale let go and told Shapley to save himself. Shapley refused, and he managed to get them both to shore. Shapley became the first US marine to receive the navy's Silver Star Medal for his heroism.

On the USS Arizona

The USS *Arizona* and six other battleships were moored in Battleship Row, a shallow harbor between Oahu and the smaller Ford Island. Just after 8:00 a.m., several men on the USS *Arizona* heard a strange buzz in the distance. They spotted airplanes in the sky, but most assumed it was a practice run from Hickam Field, the US Army air base at Pearl Harbor.

Moments later, the first bombs dropped. Black smoke billowed above the airfield. "That is the best g****** drill the army air force has ever put on!" remarked one sailor, thinking the airplanes were dropping some kind of powder to simulate an attack.[9] It immediately became apparent it was not a simulation.

PEARL HARBOR

RALEIGH

UTAH

CURTISS

FORD ISLAND

NEVADA

VESTAL

ARIZONA

WEST VIRGINIA

TENNESSEE

OKLAHOMA

MARYLAND

CALIFORNIA

HELENA

OGLALA

HONOLULU

N

W   E

S

SHAW

HELM

DOWNES

PENNSYLVANIA

CASSIN

• HOSPITAL POINT

UNDAMAGED SHIPS

DAMAGED OR SUNK SHIPS

The Japanese target was the harbor, home of the Pacific Fleet the United States depended on to defend its Pacific territories and the West Coast of the country. Seven battleships and 162 other ships were in the harbor.[10] They included repair vessels, such as the USS *Vestal*, which was tied next to the USS *Arizona*, as well as everything from cruisers to tankers to a hospital ship. The three aircraft carriers stationed in Pearl Harbor were out to sea.

Man Your Battle Stations!

The USS *Arizona* crew scrambled to their battle stations. They could now see the red circles on the attacking planes, the rising-sun symbol of the Japanese. They could see the faces of the Japanese pilots as they flew low to strafe the decks with machine-gun fire or drop torpedoes. Exploding bombs and tearing metal deafened the crews, and black smoke rose from fires as bombs hit their marks. Observers from the USS *Arizona* watched as the USS *Tennessee* and the USS *West Virginia* took hits. The USS *Oklahoma*, hit with eight torpedoes, rolled over in the water. A ninth torpedo hit the *Oklahoma* as it sank.

The battleships, packed in the harbor, could not maneuver. The USS *Nevada* made a run for the sea, trying to get out through the narrow harbor entrance. The Japanese pilots spotted the attempt to flee and went after the ship. The *Nevada's* captain, taking heavy fire and fearing the ship would be sunk and block the harbor entrance, steered the ship toward the shore and

⚓ *A view of Battleship Row after the attack shows massive destruction of the sunken and burning USS* Arizona, center, *the USS* Tennessee, left, *and the USS* West Virginia, far left.

grounded it on the beach. The antiaircraft gunners dared not fire at the low-flying torpedo planes swooping down over the harbor for fear of hitting their own ships.

Within minutes, the USS *Arizona* was hit. Men fell, wounded by machine-gun fire or shrapnel, and their fellow crewmen pulled them to safety. Bombs rocked the battleship, but it was well protected with steel plates. Then one bomb's armor-piercing shell penetrated the steel decks into the magazine. The resulting explosion ignited more than 1 million pounds (454,000 kg) of gunpowder, which became a fireball shooting 500 feet (150 m) into the air.[11] The tremendous battleship lifted into the air and then, within minutes, its keel cracked, and it sank to the ocean floor. The part of the ship that remained above water in the shallow harbor was on fire, with burning oil leaking into the water and flowing toward the other ships. The surviving crew of the USS *Arizona* continued to fight the fires while crews on the surrounding ships worked to stop the flaming inferno from igniting their own ships.

15

⚓ *In response to a possible war in Cuba in the late 1800s, the US Navy formed the Flying Squadron, a fleet that included the navy's most modern vessels of the time.*

Chapter 2

THE DREADNOUGHTS

The attack on Pearl Harbor may have been a surprise to many Americans, but it was not a surprise to the US government. Tension had been rising between the United States and Japan for dominance in the Pacific for more than four decades.

In 1898, the United States had come to the defense of Cubans seeking independence from Spain. The United States defeated Spain in the Spanish-American War (1898) and gained the territories of Guam and Puerto Rico. It also took sovereignty in the Philippines. Later that year, the United States also annexed the Territory of

17

⚓ *The first modern battleship in the US Navy's fleet, the USS* Indiana *(BB-1), was officially put into service in 1895.*

Hawaii. These new lands represented a fundamental shift in the United States. The nation now had a worldwide empire to defend, as well as hundreds of miles of coastline.

Building a Navy

Empires needed navies, and the United States joined the competition to build a fleet that could compete with naval powers such as Germany, Japan, and Britain. After the Spanish-American War, many in government clamored for more battleships. These heavily armored warships with large guns joined the US fleet at a steady pace.

New technology in the early 1900s fueled the call for more battleships. Supporters of a strong US Navy wanted to build at least two new battleships a year. They would incorporate new gun design and stronger armament, which also meant larger and more costly ships. Many in Congress resisted the call for more money to build these bigger battleships.

18

The First USS Arizona

The USS *Arizona* was not the first US ship to have the name USS *Arizona*. The previous USS *Arizona* was an iron-hulled ship built in 1859 for commercial purposes. In 1862, in the midst of the Civil War (1861–1865), Confederates seized the ship and used it to smuggle goods past Union ships. Ten months later, the USS *Montgomery* recaptured the USS *Arizona* and put it into service for the Union. In 1865, the original USS *Arizona* accidentally caught fire and was destroyed.

The Battleship Debate

A debate ensued about the appropriate size of guns and armor for new battleships. Battleship design was moving more to the use of all-big-gun design. This meant smaller-caliber guns were being replaced by 10-inch (25 cm), 12-inch (30 cm), and even-larger guns.

Opponents of the new battleships believed smaller guns could be maneuvered and fired more quickly. They had a flatter trajectory, making them easier to aim. However, their range was shorter than that of larger guns, and the shells could not penetrate the heavy armor of some of the new battleships. Proponents of the new battleships noted that it didn't make any difference how fast a gun fired if it couldn't reach its target or cause any damage when it made a hit.

Larger guns carried heavy shells that went a greater distance. Battleships with large guns could fight at a greater distance from other ships and from the submarines that prowled the seas. Submarines became significant during World War I (1914–1918) as German submarines, called U-boats, were used to destroy British and US ships carrying supplies. U-boats sank 5,000 ships during the war.[1]

The big-gun ships also had more steel-plated armor to protect them. This armor added substantial weight to the ship, which was already weighed down with massive guns, fuel, and gunpowder. Extra weight slowed the ship and increased fuel use. But in the end, the all-big-gun argument, known as "all or nothing" protection, was adopted.

Bigger and Better

By the 1910s, the world had become unstable. In Europe, tension rose as Germany sought to expand its influence. In the Pacific and Asia, conflicts rose between the United States and Japan. The United States needed to show strength through military and naval power. A tremendous new battleship would show the world that the United States was ready to defend itself.

To show its military power, US government leaders ordered several new ships, including the USS *Arizona*, in 1913. At the time it was built, the USS *Arizona* was the largest battleship in the world. Officially, the USS *Arizona* would be known as Battleship 39 (BB-39) because it was the thirty-ninth battleship of the US fleet. Unofficially, the battleship was known as a dreadnought.

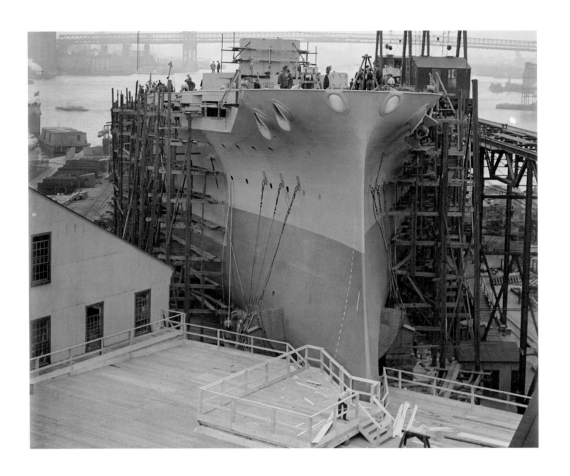

⚓ *The USS* Arizona *took 16 months to complete.*

Dreadnoughts were a special type of battleship developed at the turn of the 1900s. They were named after the first of this type of battleship, HMS *Dreadnought*, which was built for the British navy in 1906. Dreadnoughts were a revolutionary step forward in naval sea power. Battleships in the past had a mix of gun sizes, whereas the dreadnoughts had all big guns placed on turrets above the deck. The turrets could be adjusted to fire the big guns in different directions and at different angles.

Early dreadnoughts were powered by coal burned in boilers. This produced steam to drive a piston back and forth. Turbines, which are fanlike machines that generate electricity, gradually replaced the pistons. Although still driven by steam, turbines gave the ships more speed. They could outrun other ships and, increasingly more important, they could protect supply ships from the submarines. They were heavily armored with steel plates to protect against torpedo attacks.

A Super-Dreadnought

Construction on the USS *Arizona* began on March 16, 1914. The USS *Arizona* was built at the Brooklyn Navy Yard in Brooklyn, New York, at a cost of $13 million.[2] There was a ceremonial opening of assembly when five boys, sons of navy officers, inserted bolts into the first steel plates. When building a new ship, the shipyard ran 24 hours a day and employed 70,000 people.[3]

Last of the Super-Dreadnoughts

The USS *Arizona* and the USS *Pennsylvania* were the last of the super-dreadnoughts to be built. Other dreadnought classes followed, but as air power became more important in fighting wars, the United States focused on building aircraft carriers. Although large battleships were still built, they became increasingly less important. Today, only one dreadnought remains, the USS *Texas*, moored along the Houston Ship Channel as a memorial.

Diagram of the USS *Arizona*, 1918

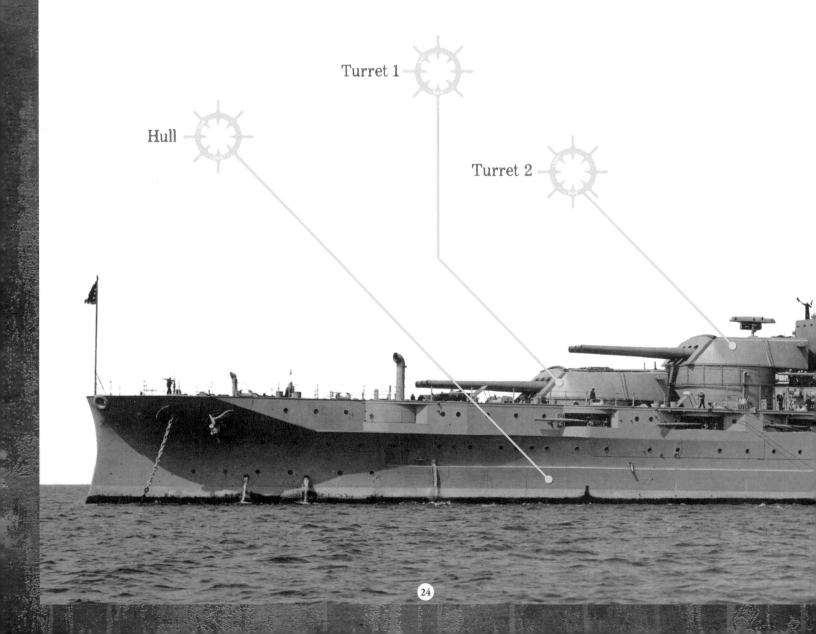

Hull

Turret 1

Turret 2

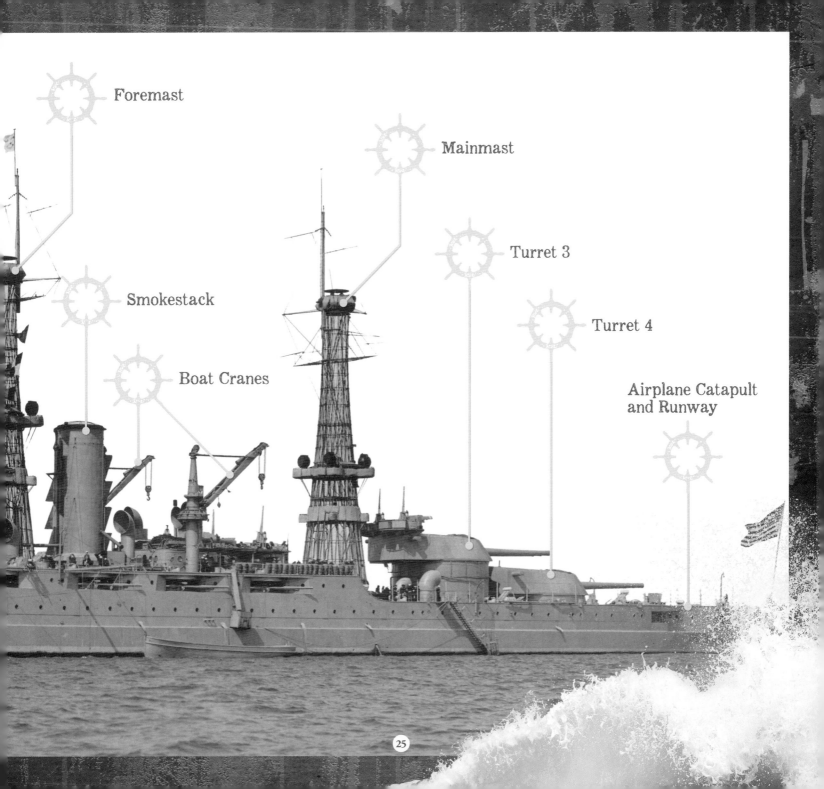

Foremast

Mainmast

Smokestack

Turret 3

Turret 4

Boat Cranes

Airplane Catapult
and Runway

25

The USS *Arizona* was built in the tradition of the dreadnoughts, but it was also bigger and better than dreadnoughts built before it—a super-dreadnought. The massive ship boasted 12 14-inch (36 cm) guns placed in four turrets. The USS *Arizona* also had 22 five-inch (13 cm) guns, four antiaircraft guns, and two torpedo launchers. To power these weapons, the USS *Arizona* carried 1 million pounds (454,000 kg) of gunpowder in its magazine.[4]

The USS *Arizona* was also designed to carry three floatplanes. The planes were used for reconnaissance, to return target coordinates, and for mail service when the ship was at sea. A gunner team launched the planes by setting off an explosive charge set behind the plane. The pressure pushed the plane down a long ramp, giving the plane enough speed to take off. When the airplane returned, the ship steered in a zigzag course to smooth the waves for a water landing. Then the plane landed on its floats, and a crane lifted it back aboard.

Another innovation on the USS *Arizona* was its fuel source. Not only was the battleship driven by four turbines, it also burned oil to fuel its boilers instead of coal. Oil had several advantages. It burned more efficiently, giving the ship more speed. It was cleaner than coal, so it did not produce black smoke that could give away the battleship's position to the enemy. It was easier to load oil through a hose than to shovel coal, and the ship could be refueled at sea. The United States was the only major power that had enough domestic oil that it would not have to buy fuel from foreign sources.

I Christen Thee ...

On June 19, 1915, approximately 75,000 people crowded the Brooklyn Navy Yard to watch the launch of the USS *Arizona*.[5] Franklin D. Roosevelt, the future president who was at that time the assistant secretary of the navy, presided over the ceremony. The ship was named after the country's newest state, Arizona, which had been admitted in 1912.

Seventeen-year-old Esther Ross, a pharmacist's daughter from Prescott, Arizona, was honored with the task of christening the new battleship, following the tradition of breaking a bottle of champagne on the bow. Ross used two bottles, one of sparkling wine and the other of water from Roosevelt Lake in Arizona. She released the bottles, held by ropes, and they smashed against the ship's hull.

The ship then moved down the slipways, slick with 30,000 pounds (13,600 kg) of grease, into the water as the crowd cheered.[6] The USS *Arizona* was far from finished. Workers would

Honoring Arizona

The people of Arizona were proud to have the new battleship named for their state. Following tradition, the state raised $9,000 to purchase an 87-piece set of silver for the captain's quarters.[7] The set had elaborate carvings of mermaids and Neptune astride dolphins to honor the sea. Carvings of saguaro cacti, the Grand Canyon, and Roosevelt Dam, which had been completed in 1911, represented the state.

27

spend another 15 months installing engines, turrets, masts, and other machinery, as well as riveting on the heavy armor plating.

On October 17, 1916, the navy officially put the USS *Arizona* into active service as part of the US fleet. The USS *Arizona* took a shakedown cruise to Guantanamo Bay, Cuba, to test its performance. Then the USS *Arizona* returned to the shipyard for repairs and alterations. On April 3, 1917, only three days before the United States entered World War I, the USS *Arizona* arrived at Norfolk Navy Base in Virginia, ready for war.

World War I

Although the USS *Arizona* was a state-of-the-art battleship, it did not see action during the war. Fuel oil was not as available in the United Kingdom as in the United States, so older coal-burning ships were dispatched to aid the war effort across the Atlantic Ocean. Some of the USS *Arizona*'s smaller guns were taken to use on ships defending the Atlantic supply lines.

Operating out of Norfolk, the USS *Arizona* patrolled the East Coast. The crew never had to fire its guns at an enemy. The ship's first major assignment was to accompany President Woodrow Wilson's ship when he attended the Paris Peace Conference in 1919. The USS *Arizona* returned to the United States, carrying 238 returning veterans, and entered New York Harbor in time for the great homecoming celebration.[8]

⚓ *In November 1916, the* USS Arizona *made its maiden voyage from the East River in New York to Hampton Roads, Virginia.*

⚓ *Crew members of the* USS Arizona *pose for a photograph with President Herbert Hoover,* seated, center front, *in March 1931.*

Chapter 3

A SAILOR'S LIFE

The USS *Arizona* carried a complement of 1,731 enlisted men and officers.[1] Many of the crew members came from small towns. Jobs were scarce for young men, especially in many farming communities, and the navy offered not only a paycheck but also an opportunity to see the world. Most had never seen an ocean, much less a mighty battleship.

The sheer size of the USS *Arizona* awed most sailors who reported for duty, but they soon found conditions on board the ship were cramped. Most of the men slept in canvas hammocks, tied

An All-Male Crew

The USS *Arizona* had an all-male crew. The average age of the men was 19 years old.[2] Although they served in the navy and marine corps as nurses and other noncombat roles, women were not allowed to serve on noncombat ships until 1978 and on combat ships until 1993.

approximately six feet (2 m) above the steel deck. They quickly learned the secret of putting sticks in between the ropes at the end to spread the hammock. This kept the canvas from closing around them like a cocoon and made it flatter so they wouldn't tumble out. The hammocks were taken down and stowed during the day to make room for tables or other equipment.

Each day began at 5:30 a.m. The men woke up, stowed their hammocks, and showered. Breakfast was at 6:30. Aboard the USS *Arizona*, navy beans were served every Sunday and Wednesday morning. At sea, food was generally dehydrated or canned: powdered milk, dehydrated eggs and potatoes, and Spam. There was plenty of ketchup to douse everything. Meals were served family style on white dishes with metal flatware.

When they met up with a reefer, or refrigerated cargo ship, they had fresh beef for a few days. In port, boats went ashore to pick up fresh fruits and vegetables. The lucky crewmen who had liberty could visit local restaurants, if they had the money, or buy a hot dog from a vendor for a dime.

⚓ *Sailors on the USS* Arizona *in the late 1920s sweep the deck to keep the ship in good working condition.*

Maintaining the Ship

The day's work began at 8:00 a.m., when the color guard raised the flag and the band played the national anthem. The battleship required constant cleaning and maintenance. The wooden teak deck needed special care to manage the effects of salt water. The newest crew members often had the task of swabbing and holystoning the deck. This meant pushing a heavy stone over the deck to smooth it and then washing the deck.

33

⚓ *Navy divers aboard the USS* Arizona *performed many jobs, from repair work to classified missions.*

The metal of the ship also required upkeep. Barnacles grew on the submerged parts of the ship. Sailors had to scrape off the barnacles to prevent drag, which would slow the ship. They scraped and repainted the ship regularly to prevent corrosion from exposure to salt water. When in port, men hung over the sides suspended by ropes to reach the vast stretches of metal plating. During the first year in Pearl Harbor, the men painted the entire fleet three times.[3]

Inspection

Fridays were field days, or days to clean the ship for the captain's inspection on Saturday. Everything had to be shipshape, which meant every surface of the ship was pristine. One sailor stationed on the USS *Arizona* recounted his experience during one inspection. He climbed on a desk to dust and polish an overhead pipe, shined the linoleum desktop until it shown, and even opened the file cabinet and touched up the paint in the drawers.

The sailor was so certain of his good work that he thought he would get a pass for liberty that night for sure. As Captain Franklin Van Valkenburgh inspected the office, the sailor stood at attention. Van Valkenburgh ran a white glove over the overhead pipe. He opened the file cabinet. Then, he looked around and flipped a switch on the wall. The fan over the door stopped, revealing a line of grease and dirt along the outer edge of the fan blades. The sailor was crestfallen. He would be staying on board that night.

Jobs aboard Ship

Sailors had a variety of jobs on the USS *Arizona*. Unskilled new recruits might work polishing brass or airing mattresses. Moving up in rank, recruits might work in the mess kitchens. They had to haul 100-pound (45 kg) sacks of flour from the scullery, where it was stored, to the kitchen or bakery on a different deck. Three times a day they put up tables, set them with plates and utensils, and then hauled huge pots of food to feed the crew. Then there was cleanup: the dishes scraped and taken to the dishwasher, tables put down, and floors mopped. One dreaded job was burning trash, which meant feeding the garbage generated by more than 1,000 men into an incinerator.

More experienced men took four-hour stints standing watch or helping steer the ship. Others were assigned to a turret as part of a team that would fire the big guns. One crewman would roll out the shell and use a mechanical device to ram it into the barrel. Four bags of powder were loaded next. The primer went in last. Then the breech was closed, sealing shut the big gun. Others then had to use the coordinates provided from the conning tower to aim and fire. Meanwhile, crewmen were bringing up more shells and powder from below.

Gunners also fired the catapult that launched the seaplanes into the air. The USS *Arizona* did not have radar, so crew members depended on the conning tower, seaplanes, and balloons to spot enemy ships and relay coordinates for the guns. More-skilled jobs included engineers, navigators, and radio operators. The ship even had its own newspaper reporters, dentists, and doctors.

Time for Play

Life aboard the ship wasn't all work. The USS *Arizona* was like a floating city. There was a barber, a store, and even an ice cream parlor. The ship's band played at official events and provided entertainment for the crew. On Saturday nights, the crew might play cards or watch a movie. Officers sat in chairs to watch the movie, while enlisted men stood. Each battleship also had its own football, baseball, and rowing teams. The sports teams on the ships competed among themselves.[4]

Not all the entertainment was organized. Men competed in friendly games such as sack races and peanut races, during which a sailor pushed a peanut across the deck with his nose. Sometimes pets were brought aboard. At one time or another, the USS *Arizona* hosted parrots, monkeys, puppies, and even a crocodile. Sailors on liberty had the opportunity to see foreign ports they would never have visited in civilian life.

At 'Em Arizona

The ship's newsletter was called *At 'Em Arizona*. This was also the ship's slogan, from the common saying, "up and at 'em," meaning to get up and get prepared. The newsletter masthead stated it was "published daily aboard the ship wherever she may be."[5] The newsletter covered sporting events, the schedule of entertainment and church services, messages from officers, and other items of interest to the members of the crew.

⚓ *Sailors on the USS* Arizona *in the 1930s practice their baseball skills at sea using a makeshift batting cage.*

In the evenings, the men joined in card games or found quiet spots to read mail from home or write letters. Many enlisted men sent a large portion of their paychecks home to help their families, especially in rural areas where the Great Depression continued through the 1930s. They could not afford to go ashore to spend their money when they had younger siblings at home to help support.

Although every sailor aboard had a specific job, the entire crew, from band members to barber, were trained for battle. This was their main task, and by 1941, most believed that the time to use those skills would come soon.

The USS Arizona Band

The USS *Arizona* was known for its excellent band. The 20-member band had attended the prestigious US Navy School of Music in Washington, DC, and had been handpicked by bandmaster Fred Kinney. The talented musicians had graduated in May 1941 and joined the USS *Arizona* in June. They were an integral part of each day. They played when the flag was raised in the morning, during dinner and supper, sometimes in the evenings to entertain the crew, and at the end of the day. The entire band was killed during the December 7 attack.

Chapter 4

⚓ *In the years after World War I, the USS* Arizona *took part in practice maneuvers and provided aid to US citizens across the globe.*

PEACETIME MISSIONS

Although World War I ended in 1918, the USS *Arizona* and its crew had to stay ready to travel where they were needed. In 1919, the USS *Arizona* sailed through the Mediterranean Sea to protect Americans during a conflict between Turkey and Greece. Marines aboard the USS *Arizona* guarded the US consulate at Smyrna, a port in present-day Turkey, while US citizens and some Greek citizens sheltered aboard the ship.

In the next decade, the USS *Arizona* spent time in the Caribbean Sea, visiting several island ports and practicing maneuvers along the

East Coast. In 1921, the ship traveled through the Panama Canal for the first time for a visit to Peru and, subsequently, remained in the Pacific.

Training Exercises

The USS *Arizona* was most often used in training exercises. Target practice could be particularly harrowing for the members of the crew who pulled the targets. Sailors in a small boat would tow a platform, which served as the target. They positioned the target approximately 20 miles (32 km) from the ship. To hit such a long-range target, gunners depended on information from the conning tower to tell them the target's location. The USS *Arizona* would take aim and fire. Those towing the target would hear the shells scream as they neared the target, then the whoosh of the hit would rock the smaller boat. Fortunately for the target crews, the ship rated excellent on accuracy for its big guns.

Target practice also meant cleaning the big guns. The barrels had to be brushed clean and oiled. The smallest member of the team got the job of climbing down the barrel to clean inside.

Then, there were drills for all types of scenarios. Crew members had to know what to do if the electricity failed or radio communication went down. What would they do if the turret commander were wounded?

⚓ *The USS* Arizona *underwent modernization at the Norfolk Navy Yard between May 1929 and March 1931.*

Updates

To keep the USS *Arizona* in top shape, the navy took it out of commission and sent it to the Norfolk Navy Yard in Virginia. Beginning in 1929, crews spent nearly two years modernizing the USS *Arizona*'s equipment, weapons, and power sources.

Crews installed new tripod masts that housed the control equipment for the ship's big guns. Thicker deck armor was added to protect critical areas of the ship. Blisters were added

The USS Arizona by the Numbers

HULL NUMBER	BB-39
COMPLEMENT	1,731
CONSTRUCTION STARTED	March 16, 1914
CHRISTENED	June 19, 1915
COMMISSIONED	October 17, 1917
CONSTRUCTION COST	$12,993,579.00
LENGTH	600 feet (183 m)
WIDTH	608 feet (185 m)
DISPLACEMENT	Normal load: 34,207 short tons (31,032 metric tons) Full load: 37,654 short tons (34,159 metric tons)
MAIN ARMAMENT	Twelve 14-inch (36 cm) 45-caliber guns mounted on four turrets
RANGE	34,000 yards (31,000 m)
SECONDARY ARMAMENT	Twelve 5-inch (13 cm) 51-caliber, single-mounted guns
RANGE	17,100 yards (15,600 m)
ANTIAIRCRAFT ARMAMENT	Eight 5-inch (13 cm) 25-caliber, single-mounted guns
AIRCRAFT	Three Vought OS2U Kingfishers (single engine)

for protection. These honeycomb-like metal projections on the side of the ship were supposed to detonate torpedoes and contain the explosions. Five-inch (13 cm) guns replaced the three-inch (7.6 cm) ones.

The updates made the USS *Arizona* heavier, so its power sources were updated, too. The turbines, which had had problems since the initial launch, were replaced along with the boilers. The ship fuel storage was also nearly doubled.

Fleet Problem XIII

The USS *Arizona* also participated in what the navy called Fleet Problems. These were large tactical exercises, beginning in 1923 and ending in 1940, that addressed particular situations as the navy developed new technologies and strategies. They involved large numbers of vessels and gave commanders an opportunity to determine the effectiveness of various tactics.

In 1932, Fleet Problem XIII assumed that an invading force had taken Hawaii and the navy had to take it back. Captain John Towers developed a strategy in which aircraft carriers would leave the main fleet and secretly approach the harbor to launch an air attack at dawn on a Sunday morning. The strategy took army participants, who were playing the part of the foreign invaders, completely by surprise. Captain Towers later learned from a Japanese vice admiral that the Japanese attack of December 7 was based on this idea.

The next year found the USS *Arizona* in Long Beach, California, aiding victims of the Long Beach earthquake. The ship's crew provided medical aid, supplies, and security during the cleanup.

Aircraft Carriers

The three aircraft carriers of the Pacific Fleet, the USS *Enterprise*, the USS *Lexington*, and the USS *Saratoga*, were at sea on various missions when the Japanese attacked on December 7. The majority of the US aircraft carriers were in the Atlantic Fleet because Germany was considered a greater threat than Japan. Aircraft carriers began replacing battleships before World War II because the range of airplanes carrying torpedoes or bombs flying off the carriers was much greater than the range of the big guns on the battleships. By the end of World War II, the dreadnoughts were basically obsolete.

Bigger Guns

By 1939, the USS *Arizona* was updated again. Its four massive turrets boasted even larger guns. Each one had a diameter of 14 inches (35 cm) and a barrel that stretched 52 feet (16 m). These long, powerful guns weighed 70 short tons (63.5 metric tons) each. The ship also carried smaller guns. It had twelve 5-inch (13 cm) single-mount guns, as well as eight 5-inch antiaircraft guns.[1] The increased number of antiaircraft guns was significant as more and more military expenditures of the world powers were being used for aircraft carriers and aircraft rather than battleships.

Updating ships in the US fleet was a priority amid worrisome news reports from Europe. On September 1,

46

⚓ *The sailors posing inside the gun barrels on one of the USS Arizona's turrets provide perspective on the huge size of the ship's firepower.*

1939, German forces invaded Poland, which started World War II. Britain and France came to Poland's defense, declaring war on Germany on September 3. In the United States, people were divided between those who wanted to aid its British and French allies and those who wanted to stay out of wars in Europe.

⚓ *An aerial photograph of Ford Island, Hawaii, shows US ships in formation on May 3, 1940, just after the conclusion of Fleet Problem XXI.*

Preparing for War

Though the United States remained officially neutral, its forces continued to prepare. In April 1940, the USS *Arizona* took part in Fleet Problem XXI, an exercise that simulated an attack at sea on a dispersed US fleet or an attack on Pearl Harbor by the Japanese fleet. This would be the last Fleet Problem. In June, President Franklin D. Roosevelt ordered the fleet to move its main base from California to Pearl Harbor to send a message to Japan.

The USS *Arizona* spent Christmas 1940 at Bremerton, the naval shipyard in Washington State. The weather was chilly and rainy, and the crew was tense. Rumors of war swirled as the USS *Arizona* prepared for battle. The antiaircraft guns got new, more accurate range finders. Four new machine guns were mounted high above the deck.

Anything not essential to the ship was left behind to lighten the ship's weight. This would make the ship faster and use less fuel. The captain's fancy silverware was packed and stored away. Even the radios some sailors kept for listening to music were left behind.

48

Rumors of War

As the USS *Arizona* sailed back down the Pacific coast in January 1941, the daily routines changed. Lights were extinguished at night. Extra patrols made sure watertight doors and hatches were secured. Back in Pearl Harbor, the crew was now spending more time out at sea practicing maneuvers. Gossip said that Japanese submarines prowled the area. The USS *Arizona* made one last trip to the West Coast in June, then returned to Pearl Harbor in July. Activity picked up even more during the fall.

Although the United States had remained neutral in the war, many believed US involvement in the war was unavoidable. Germany was overrunning much of Europe, and Japan was expanding throughout Asia and the South Pacific. Americans remained split between those who wanted to stay out of foreign entanglements and those who wanted to help defend US allies in Europe.

Fleet Operations Report Gone Wrong

Fleet operations could have moments of levity. A reporter from *Life* magazine covered the operations in 1940. One morning, he climbed onto a platform over the captain's bridge for a better view when a gust of wind blew the sunshade and filter off his camera. They fell near the vice admiral. The reporter was charged with "willfully, maliciously and without justifiable cause assaulting and attempting to strike with a dangerous weapon of German manufacture one Adolphus Andrews, Vice Admiral."[2] He was locked in the brig. Once everyone had a good laugh, he was set free.

An Accident

On October 22, 1941, US battleships were practicing moving in formation, zigzagging across the Pacific waters. The USS *Arizona* changed course to stay in sync with the other battleships. Visibility was poor. The USS *Oklahoma* bore down on the USS *Arizona*. The USS *Oklahoma* had not made its turn. The ships took evasive action, but it was impossible to avoid a collision.

The USS *Arizona* lurched sideways 100 feet (30 m) with a scream of tearing metal as the USS *Oklahoma* grazed its side, tearing off the protective layer of the honeycomb-like metal that was supposed to minimize torpedo attacks. The USS *Oklahoma* ripped a hole in the hull large enough to drive a truck through. The USS *Arizona* began taking on water, listing to one side. The crew scrambled to let in water on the other side to right the ship.

The sailors of the USS *Arizona* managed to stabilize the ship and temporarily patch the hole. Three days later, they returned to Pearl Harbor. The ship went to dry dock for more permanent repairs. The men stayed on board and scraped barnacles off the hull while repairs were made.

The accident was a huge disappointment to the crewmen of the ship. The USS *Arizona* had been scheduled to return to the West Coast of the United States in late November, but now they would miss the opportunity to spend Christmas at home while the ship was repaired.

Chapter 5

⚓ *Sailors stand in disbelief amid wrecked planes at the Ford Island seaplane base, watching as the USS* Shaw *explodes during the Pearl Harbor attack.*

SINKING THE USS *ARIZONA*

On December 1, 1941, the USS *Arizona* was again on maneuvers. Japanese submarines were spotted following the fleet. The USS *Arizona* returned to Pearl Harbor on December 5. Two days later, the USS *Arizona* crew woke to sounds of Japanese bombs raining down on Pearl Harbor.

All the battleships trapped in Battleship Row took increasing fire. The USS *Oklahoma* was hit and capsized. The USS *Utah* sank. The USS *Arizona*'s magazine exploded, making the ship's devastation almost unimaginable. Steel armor six inches (15 cm) thick curled like paper. The explosion blew debris and bodies thousands of feet into the air. One man from the USS *West Virginia* recalled, "I saw the [USS] *Arizona* blow up and she just rained sailors."[1] Another man remembered the scores of white sailor caps, the men's names stenciled in black, floating in the harbor.

Most of the crew members were killed instantly. Rear Admiral Isaac C. Kidd, commander of Battleship Division One, and the captain of the ship, Franklin Van Valkenburgh, had headed for the bridge when the attack began. Nothing remained of either man but their metal rings and a few metal buttons. Lieutenant Commander Samuel Glenn Fuqua, the highest-ranking officer remaining on the USS *Arizona*, took charge of evacuating the survivors who remained on the ship.

Casualties were horrendous. Many men were burned over most of their bodies. Others had been pierced by bullets or torn by shrapnel from the explosion.

Keep Fighting!

Up and down the harbor, ships were on fire. Crews manned fire hoses to try to push the burning oil away from their ships as bullets from machine guns on Japanese airplanes strafed the decks. Explosion after explosion rocked the harbor as torpedoes and bombs hit their marks. The noise from exploding shells and screaming men was deafening. The smell of oil and

Mini-Bio ⚓

Samuel Glenn *Fuqua* ⚓

US Navy Rear Admiral

Samuel Glenn Fuqua (1899–1987) received the Medal of Honor "for distinguished conduct in action, outstanding heroism, and utter disregard of his own safety above and beyond the call of duty" during the Pearl Harbor attack on December 7, 1941.[2] After being knocked unconscious by one of the first bombs dropped on the ship, he regained consciousness just before the magazine blew up. With dead and dying all around, he personally helped 70 wounded onto a boat from the hospital ship *Solace* that took them to shore. He then helped many of the shocked and wounded off the slick decks into rescue boats. His calm demeanor saved many lives, quelling the panic among the younger men, many still teenagers. Fuqua had fought in the army during World War I. His first tour of duty in the navy was aboard the USS *Arizona* from 1922 to 1923.

"Praise the Lord and Pass the Ammunition!"

Lieutenant Howell M. Forgy was a chaplain aboard the USS *New Orleans*. As a chaplain, his battle station was the sick bay, but as the bombs continued to hit Pearl Harbor he wanted to do something to help. When the electricity failed and the crew formed a line to pass the heavy shells up to the gunners by hand, he stood along the line encouraging them by saying, "Praise the Lord and pass the Ammunition!"[3] The phrase became a rallying cry during the war and was later incorporated into a famous patriotic song, "Praise the Lord and Pass the Ammunition," by Frank Loesser.

burning flesh would remain with the survivors for the rest of their lives.

As crews clambered up from below, they first stared in disbelief, then rushed to mount a defense. The Japanese airplanes flew low coming down the harbor to drop their torpedoes. It was easy to spot the red circles on their wings. Dodging the carnage made it difficult for the Americans to get teams to their guns, but within five minutes, some crews had mounted a defense. Those who did found that most of the ammunition was locked up in stores below because it was Sunday morning.

Saving Lives

On the USS *Arizona*, many men were trapped below deck or too badly wounded to climb the ladders. Their fellow crewmen risked their own lives to help them.

⚓ *An aerial view of the Pearl Harbor attack shows US antiaircraft shells bursting above the smoky wreck of the USS Arizona, center.*

Men gave their lives shining a light to guide the way to doors or opening portholes so others could escape before them.

Those on deck leaped into the water to avoid the burning ship. The water was aflame with oil. One man who had never passed his swimming test jumped anyway and found he

57

could swim. Another man had never swum underwater before but learned that skill quickly to avoid the flaming surface. Smaller boats pulled oil-covered sailors from the water as they floundered in the thick muck. Many had lost their clothes in the blast and fires. Their bare flesh was slick with oil, making it difficult to pull them out of the water. Other men swam to shore, avoiding the debris and bodies floating on the surface.

High in one of the antiaircraft directors, a metal box containing the crews that fired the guns, the gunners watched the chaos below. The men had rushed up the ladders to man the guns, one shot in the leg as he climbed, but now the ladders were useless, twisted metal. The men were too high to jump to safety. Most were severely wounded, burned by the explosion, and the fires below were turning the metal box where they were trapped into an oven.

The captain of the USS *Vestal* was Cassin Young. The USS *Vestal* was moored alongside the USS *Arizona*. Young had been blown off his ship by the blast and had to swim back to his command. Fortunately, the blast shock had sucked oxygen from the air, putting out the fire on the USS *Vestal*. A crewman saw the predicament of the men on the USS *Arizona* and, defying an order from the returned USS *Vestal* commander to move away from the burning ship, threw a line up to the men. One by one, they climbed out of the director and went hand over hand for approximately 70 feet (20 m) down the rope, clinging desperately with their charred hands to avoid falling into the flames below. The USS *Arizona* sank in nine minutes. Only 335 of the

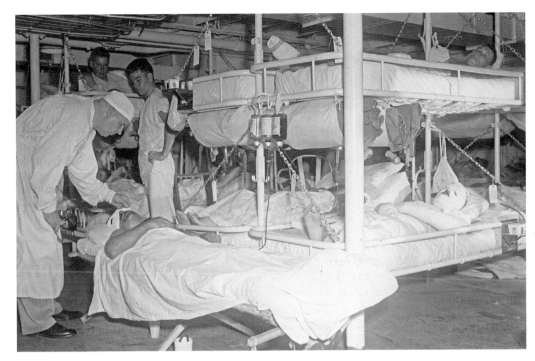

⚓ *Burned and injured patients received care aboard the hospital ship USS* Solace *following the Pearl Harbor attack.*

USS *Arizona* crewmen survived.[4] More than one-half of the naval casualties in the Pearl Harbor attack were from the USS *Arizona*. The ship lost 1,177 men.[5]

On Shore

Wounded survivors, many with severe shrapnel wounds or bad burns, were taken to hospitals. Overwhelmed, nurses treated men laid out on the lawns. They administered morphine to ease the pain, using lipstick to put an "M" on the men's foreheads so other nurses would not accidentally give them overdoses.

⚓ *All that remained of the USS* Arizona *three days after the Pearl Harbor attack was a charred, sunken shell.*

Many of the officers had families that lived nearby. Once the shock was over, the civilians in the community rushed to help. They ripped sheets for bandages and gathered medical supplies. Doctors amputated limbs, sometimes operating while patients were still on the stretchers they had been carried in on. Bodies and limbs were heaped in piles. At 9:45 a.m., less than two hours later, the triumphant Japanese pilots headed back to their carriers.

Damage to the Enemy

The Japanese did not come away from Pearl Harbor unscathed. US forces shot down 29 Japanese aircraft and sank five midget submarines. One hundred twenty-nine Japanese soldiers died in the attack, and one Japanese soldier was taken prisoner.[7]

Aftermath

At approximately 1:00 p.m., the Japanese ships left. Many of the pilots had hoped for a third strike to take out the fuel tanks and other facilities. The Japanese commanders decided to quit while they were ahead. It had been a devastating blow to the United States, and the commanders feared the cruisers that had escaped the harbor or the missing aircraft carriers would soon find them. They headed for home, leaving the Americans with the 4.5-million-barrel petroleum tank untouched and intact repair facilities that would allow them to repair the fleet and later turn the tide of the war.[6]

The attack destroyed 169 aircraft and damaged 159 others.[8] The USS *Oklahoma* had turned over and capsized. The USS *Utah* and USS *West Virginia* sank. The USS *Nevada* tried to get out of the harbor but ended up grounding on the beach. The other battleships in the harbor and the USS *Pennsylvania*, which was in dry dock, were damaged, along with several cruisers and destroyers. Casualties totaled 3,581, with 2,403 killed and 1,178 wounded, including navy personnel and civilians.[9]

Failed Japanese Subs

Part of the Japanese attack plan was to circle Pearl Harbor with submarines that would torpedo ships that tried to escape. Minisubs, smaller submarines carrying two men and two torpedoes, were launched from the submarines to penetrate the harbor. That part of the plan failed. One of the minisubs was sunk by the USS *Ward*, one ran aground, and the other three disappeared at sea—found decades later by US researchers.

The USS Arizona's Fate

Its masts leaning to one side above the ruptured deck, the USS *Arizona* burned for days, despite efforts to put out the fires. Once the twisted metal had cooled, a team was assigned to recover any remains of the crew they could find. They were given sheets and pillowcases, and they went through all the ship that remained above the water from the decks to the top of the masts. They reverently wrapped any bodies they found in sheets and put scattered body parts and bits of bone in the pillowcases. It took two days. It was a horrendous duty as the charred flesh had been exposed for days in the hot tropical sun.

Divers were sent 20 feet (6 m) below the oily waters to search for any crewmen who might have survived in pockets of air in the sunken ship. They methodically went the length of the ship sounding the hull, rapping three times with a hammer on the metal hull approximately every 25 feet (8 m) and waiting for a response. No one was found.

In late January, an attempt was made to recover the bodies of those who remained missing. Divers removed a small percentage of the total bodies, but it was dangerous and horrifying work recovering the rotting corpses through the twisted doorways and buckled metal. Even after they were recovered, it was impossible to identify the remains—DNA identification had not been developed. The navy decided the crewmen who remained missing were dead and would remain below with their ship, buried at sea.

World War II Scuba Gear

Scuba gear as we know it today had not yet been invented in 1941. Navy divers wore Mark V suits to cut holes in the hull of the USS *Oklahoma* to rescue crewmen and for salvage operations. The suit featured a large metal helmet with a hinged porthole in front. Divers breathed through a hose. It wasn't until after World War II that French navy diver and world-famous undersea explorer Jacques Cousteau and engineer Émile Gagnan invented a device for breathing compressed air underwater.

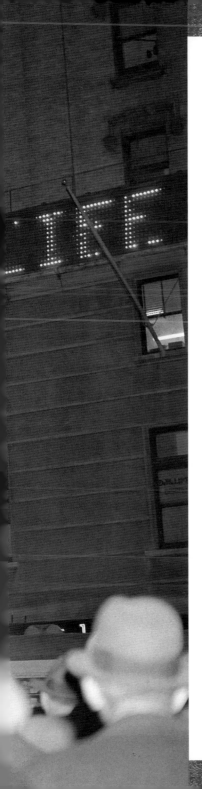

⚓ *Crowds gathered in New York's Times Square early in the evening on December 7, 1941, to read the news of the attack as it flashed on an electric bulletin board.*

Chapter 6

AN ANGRY COUNTRY

At approximately 1:30 p.m. on December 7, 1941, Secretary of the Navy Frank Knox interrupted President Roosevelt in his study, today known as the Oval Office, to announce that Japan had attacked Pearl Harbor. As the president received confirmation and details on the telephone, his wife, Eleanor, walked in. She later described the president as "deadly calm."[1]

Within hours, Japan had attacked US facilities in the Philippines. It also attacked Hong Kong and Malaysia, bringing the United Kingdom and Canada into the war against Japan. Japanese military leaders knew they had to inflict maximum damage before the United States got back on its feet.

Details Emerge

As the day wore on and news began arriving from Hawaii, reporters flocked to the press room. People gathered outside the White House to watch the parade of dignitaries filing inside. Rumors were rampant.

News traveled much slower in 1941 than it does today, but word of the attack on December 7 soon got out. President Roosevelt tried to keep the number of casualties and the extent of the damage quiet. He did not want to provide Japan with details of the success of the attack, and he did not want people in the United States to panic. People stayed glued to their radios as details unfolded. They gathered before the ticker in Times Square. Some newspapers managed to go to print the same day.

Even President Roosevelt had little information. A report at 3:50 p.m. informed the president that the USS *Oklahoma* had capsized and the USS *Tennessee* was on fire. It did not mention the USS *Arizona*, so President Roosevelt did not know the extent of the casualties. A report at 7:10 p.m. gave a more detailed account on the condition of the battleships but simply said that the USS *Arizona* "was hit by torpedoes or aerial bombs and she . . . is capsized."[2]

⚓ *President Franklin D. Roosevelt speaks to Congress the day after the Japanese attack on Pearl Harbor.*

Later that evening, the Japanese formally declared war on the United States. President Roosevelt consulted with congressional leaders, his cabinet, and military advisers. Before retiring for the night, he dictated a speech to deliver to Congress the next day. He would ask Congress to formally declare war on Japan.

Monday Morning

On the morning of December 8, President Roosevelt learned the full extent of the damage, including the horrendous destruction of the USS *Arizona*. He left for the US Capitol under heavy guard. Fearing an assassination attempt, the Secret Service brought the bulletproof limousine that the Treasury Department had confiscated from notorious gangster Al Capone to use as a presidential limousine.

As President Roosevelt was driven the short distance, he practiced his speech. He reread one line, "a date which will live in world history," that he had crossed out so the line read, "a date which will live in infamy."[3] It became one of the most famous quotes from World War II. At the Capitol, the president's eldest son, James, assisted his father out of the car and helped him balance on the stiff leg braces he had to wear to walk.

At 12:30 p.m., President Roosevelt delivered his speech to a joint session of Congress. The speech was carried via radio to the American people. Congress quickly voted to declare war against Japan, with only one person voting no. Four days later, Germany declared war on the United States. The United States was going to have to fight a war on two fronts.

Anticipated Attack?

Although the sneak attack on December 7 took the country by surprise, the United States had anticipated an attack by Japan. In 1931, Japan had invaded Manchuria, and the conflict had become a full-scale war between Japan and China by 1937. Japanese war atrocities solidified public opinion in the West to align with China, and Western countries began sending supplies

Mini-Bio ⚓

Franklin D. Roosevelt

President of the United States

Franklin D. Roosevelt (1882–1945) served as president of the United States from 1933 to his death in 1945, leading the country through two of its most trying crises, the Great Depression and World War II. His calm demeanor, shown to citizens during his fireside chats—radio talks directed at the people of the United States—gave Americans a sense of trust. He helped still the fear during the Great Depression, convincing people the United States could overcome any problem if they all worked together and saying during his first inauguration, "The only thing we have to fear is fear itself."[4] Roosevelt contracted polio at age 39 and afterward often used a wheelchair. Not wanting to show weakness, he wore leg braces that went from ankle to hip to walk when in public.

⚓ *President Roosevelt signs the declaration of war against Germany on December 11, 1941.*

to support China's defense. Japan then attempted to control these supply lines, invading French Indochina in 1940. In retaliation, the United States imposed trade sanctions and then an embargo in July of 1940, halting supplies of airplanes and aviation fuel to Japan. The Japanese military determined that a surprise attack was the only way to prevent US involvement in Southeast Asia.

Rumors began that the Japanese were planning to attack the West Coast. The people residing on the coast lived in fear, vigilantly turning out lights and covering windows at night to create a blackout so as not to provide Japanese airplanes or submarines with targets. Suspicion centered on Japanese Americans who lived in the United States who could potentially be saboteurs or signal ships and submarines offshore.

Japanese Internment

After the attack on Pearl Harbor, the US government perceived all people of Japanese descent living within the United States as a threat to national security. The military relocated approximately 120,000 Japanese-Americans to ten remote internment camps throughout the country. The camps were crowded, and prisoners slept in barracks. Armed guards prevented people from leaving the camps. Many Japanese-Americans felt betrayed by their country. The US government finally closed the last camp in March 1946, six months after the war had ended.

Enlist!

People across the United States were horrified and shocked—and they were angry. In many people's minds, the surprise attack showed Japan to be a country without honor. This dirty trick went against the honesty and forthrightness of many average Americans. People wanted to do something.

Hundreds of thousands of young men lined up at recruiting stations to enlist. Some stations stayed open 24 hours a day to accommodate the long lines. Old men, some veterans of World War I, were turned away, told they were too old to fight. Teenagers, as young as 15 years old, lied about their age to enter the war. Still, it would take more than volunteers to win this war. The United States had a draft, but it was limited to one million men and women. Once war was declared, this limit was lifted. Those in industries considered essential to the war effort, such as oil production and farming, were exempt from the draft.

Americans Rally

People who couldn't enlist supported the effort by buying war bonds—called defense bonds before the attack on Pearl Harbor. The government enlisted the help of advertising agencies and celebrities to encourage people to defend the United States and democracy by buying bonds to support the war effort. The minisubmarine captured at Pearl Harbor was toured around the country to help sell bonds, and posters declared "Remember Pearl Harbor."

People who couldn't afford a bond could buy war stamps for as little as a dime. These could be saved and traded for bonds. Schools, towns, and other organizations launched campaigns to

AVENGE PEARL HARBOR

OUR BULLETS WILL DO IT.

⚓ *The US War Production Board used the Pearl Harbor attack as a rallying cry for support of the war effort.*

72

help fund the defense of the United States. The war bond campaign was the most successful advertising campaign in history. Half of the US population bought war bonds, raising $185.7 billion for the war effort.[5]

The military also needed oil, rubber for tires, and food and equipment for the troops. Oil and other essential commodities were rationed. People planted home gardens, billed as Victory Gardens, so more nonperishable food could go to the troops. Factories that made consumer goods retooled to manufacture guns, ammunition, and tanks. As men left to fight on the European and Pacific fronts, women took responsibility for raising families and filled the factory jobs. By the end of the war, nearly 25 percent of married women worked outside the home, a cultural shift that continued to grow in the following decades.[6]

The country united behind the rallying cry, "Remember Pearl Harbor!" The USS *Arizona*, where more than half of the deaths had occurred on that horrendous day, became a symbol for the spirit and determination that drove the country forward.

Buy Bonds!

The United States spent approximately $296 billion ($4 trillion in today's dollars) fighting World War II.[7] The government sold war bonds to raise money for tanks, supplies, uniforms, and everything else needed to fight the war. Buying a war bond was a way for citizens to loan money to the government. Bonds earned interest and could be cashed in within a specific period, usually ten years. For instance, a bond purchased from the government for $18.75 could be redeemed for $25 after ten years.[8]

Salvage and Repair

Meanwhile, at Pearl Harbor, salvage and repair began even before the smoke cleared. Parts were salvaged from the heavily damaged airplanes and ships to repair less damaged vessels. All battleships other than the USS *Arizona* and USS *Utah* would rejoin the fleet.

Captain Homer Wallin was put in charge of the USS *Arizona* salvage efforts. A dive team and the ordnance groups dismantled turrets 3 and 4 and removed the 14-inch (35.6 cm) shells. Cranes removed many of the guns, which were sent to be refurbished. Anything that could be used from the USS *Arizona* was salvaged. Guns, ammunition, and machinery were saved. The dive team also salvaged the 12-foot (3.6 m) range finder and 36-inch (91 cm) searchlights. The two main gun turrets that were left were removed along with the guns from turret 2. The stern aircraft crane and conning tower were cut away. Inside the ship, the safe was opened and the money stored for payroll was removed, much of it in $2 bills.

Once everything that could be salvaged was removed, the navy determined that the remaining wreck did not pose a threat to navigation in the harbor. It would be costly and time consuming to raise the remains of the ship—and the navy needed that money and time to fight a war. The USS *Arizona* and those buried with it were left where they lay.

⚓ *Members of the diving crew emerge from the sunken USS* Arizona *after removing elements of the ship's armament and other items for reuse.*

The military at Pearl Harbor worked at a feverish rate to restore the base to action. Within weeks, many of the ships and airplanes were active. Within seven months, the United States turned the tide of the war in the South Pacific at the Battle of Midway. US troops relentlessly drove the Japanese back toward Tokyo. On August 6, 1945, the United States dropped the first nuclear bomb on Hiroshima, Japan. Three days later the United States dropped a second nuclear bomb on the city of Nagasaki, Japan. Japan surrendered on August 15. More than 200,000 people died in the two attacks.[9]

⚓ *In May 1945, sailors celebrated the end of World War II in Europe after Germany's surrender.*

LEST WE FORGET

The attack at Pearl Harbor was a seminal event in history. It changed the way Americans thought of their country—and how the world viewed the United States. Before the war, the country had been divided between those who wanted the United States to remain isolated from the battles raging in the rest of the world and those who wanted to help defend US allies. The attack on Pearl Harbor brought the country together in a fervor of patriotism and a willingness to work together for a greater future.

However, as after all historic events, many people moved on after the war. Those who witnessed the events at Pearl Harbor on December 7, 1941, seldom talked about what they saw or endured. Many had nightmares or horrid recollections of the incidents. Years later, one survivor was at the beach and rushed into the water to save a child. He froze as the memories of swimming through the blood, bodies, and flaming oil came back. The child was saved by onlookers, but the man never went into the ocean again.

At that time, the medical community and people in general did not know about post-traumatic stress disorder (PTSD). The survivors returned to their homes after the war and most had families, but they did not tell their stories to their children. The postwar generation thrived in a booming economy in a country that was now a world power.

Recognition

The USS *Arizona* remained resting at the bottom of the harbor. Passing ships paid homage to those who died and lay interred there, but it wasn't until 1949 that the Pacific War Memorial Commission organized plans for a permanent memorial. The next year, the USS *Arizona* was symbolically recommissioned when a flagpole was erected on the ship. Today, the USS *Arizona* is treated as part of the fleet, flying the ship's flag at half-staff when other ships of the fleet do.

⚓ *On average, 4,000 visitors take the ferry each day to the USS Arizona Memorial, which spans the ship's sunken wreckage.*

In 1958, President Dwight Eisenhower allowed fund-raising to begin for construction of a memorial. The navy wanted a bridge-like memorial spanning the sunken wreck. The design selected was submitted by Alfred Preis, an Austrian-born American who had spent three and a half months in a US internment camp in Hawaii after the Pearl Harbor bombing.

Elvis Presley's Contribution

The money for the monument, $500,000, was to be raised through private donations. The first year, approximately 20 percent of the funds were raised, but then donations stalled.[1]

Alfred Preis

Alfred Preis, an Austrian-born American, designed the USS *Arizona* Memorial. Fleeing the Nazi takeover in Austria, he arrived with his wife in Honolulu in 1939 at just 28 years old and went to work for an architectural firm. He rose at the company quickly, but that changed on December 7. The next night, he was forced into an internment camp with other German, Austrian, and Japanese Americans. By the time he was released three and a half months later, he had lost everything. He started his own business, which quickly became successful, and later founded the Hawaii State Foundation for Culture and the Arts, which promotes public art and art education.

Rock-and-roll star Elvis Presley, whose own career had stalled during his stint in the army, volunteered to do a concert to help raise funds.

On March 25, 1961, Presley put on a concert, and it was a huge success. Presley performed his most famous songs, and the teens in the crowd went wild. The 45-minute concert brought in $47,000, and additional donations continued flowing in. The entire amount needed to build the memorial was raised within the next five months—with a few federal dollars added—including $40,000 raised through the sale of models of the USS *Arizona*.[2]

The Memorial

With the needed funds secured, construction on the memorial began in 1960. One hundred and eighty-four feet (56 m) long, the concrete structure straddles the midsection of the wreck like a floating bridge.[3] Parts of

⚓ *Elvis Presley performs at Pearl Harbor's Bloch Arena to raise money for the USS Arizona Memorial.*

the ship were cut away to provide space for the pillars that would support the monument. The shape of the memorial, high at both ends and sunken in the middle, symbolizes the low point in history when the United States was unprepared and attacked. No part of the memorial touches the wreck. Texas congressman Olin E. Teague, a World War II veteran and chair of the House Veterans' Committee, formally dedicated the memorial on Memorial Day in 1962. It then became open to the public.

For many, a visit to the memorial is an emotional experience. Visitors arrive by ferry at a dock that displays one of the USS *Arizona*'s anchors. They go into the Entry Room and move into the Assembly Hall. The atmosphere is reverent and quiet, as is fitting for a war cemetery.

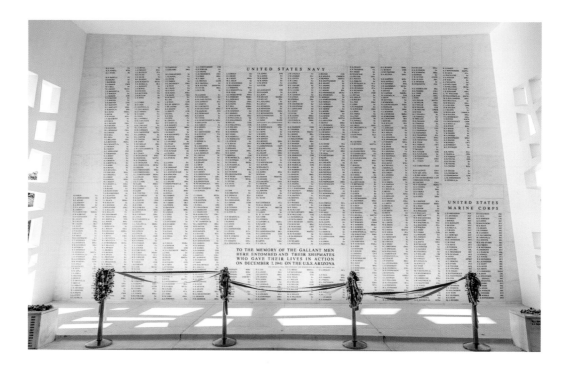

The Shrine Room's engraved marble slabs honor the sailors who gave their lives on the USS Arizona.

The central area is reserved for ceremonies and general observation. There are seven tall windows along each side of the memorial, symbolizing the date of the attack. Seven more open to the sky. Together, the 21 windows symbolize a permanent 21-gun salute.

People gather at the rails surrounding a large hole cut in the floor that allows a view of the ship's deck below the water. Visitors often drop flowers or coins here in remembrance. The last section, the Shrine Room, has a marble wall engraved with the names of those killed. Here, people search for the names of friends, loved ones, ancestors, or simply take in the magnitude of the number of young men who lost their lives on the ship.

A War Grave

The memorial spans a war grave for the 1,102 men who lie below and the survivors who have chosen to join their comrades after they die.[4] In 1982, the first group of approximately 40 survivors of the USS *Arizona* who have chosen to be buried on the ship was interred.[5]

For those who choose to be buried there, the navy holds a special ceremony on the memorial. There is a funeral, a two-bell ceremony, and a rifle salute, and a flag is presented to the family. The two-bell ceremony is the tradition of tolling the bells to mark the death of a sailor. Traditionally, two bells mark the end of the day on a ship. The ceremony ends with the playing of "Taps."

As the final notes drift across the harbor, an urn with the ashes of the deceased is given to navy divers. The divers take the urn below to a slot, approximately 6 inches by 5 feet (15 cm x 1.5 m), that opens into an area called the barbette below the location of gun turret 4. The urns are placed into the slot, where they slide into the ship to lay at rest with the fallen sailors.

Buried at Sea

The USS *Utah* is also a war grave with 54 of the 58 crewmen killed on December 7 still entombed in the ship.[6] There are also the ashes of a baby on the ship. She had died two days earlier and her father had brought her ashes aboard to be scattered at sea. They went down with the ship. The USS *Arizona* is the only venue where survivors of the attack can be interred with their comrades. Survivors of other venues of the Pearl Harbor attack can elect to have their ashes scattered where their ship was moored.

The names of those interred since the sinking of the ship are engraved on a plaque in the Shrine Room.

Survivors

Over time, survivors of the attack have become more comfortable telling their stories. Invited by Mark Ferris, editor of the *Gardena Tribune* and a Pearl Harbor survivor who was at Hickam Field, a few of the survivors began getting together for informal dinners in 1954. They found that it was much easier to speak with others who had shared their experience.

Pearl Harbor Survivors Organization

The Pearl Harbor Survivors Organization was chartered by Congress in 1958. However, by 2011, there were so few survivors left that the organization was disbanded. A new organization, Sons and Daughters of Pearl Harbor Survivors, was established in 1972 to carry forward the legacy of their parents.

The gatherings grew and, in 1962, more than 1,000 survivors met in Long Beach and officially founded the Pearl Harbor Survivors Organization. The organization's mission was to make sure Pearl Harbor, and the lessons learned there, was not forgotten and that the stories of the heroes of that day did not die. In time, membership grew to 18,000 members.[7]

The USS *Arizona* Memorial hosted many reunions through the years. It was difficult for survivors to return to Pearl Harbor but, in time, many found some peace

⚓ *Pearl Harbor survivors gathered at the memorial for a ceremony on the 74th anniversary of the attack.*

seeing the site and speaking with others who shared their experience. But by the seventy-fifth anniversary of the attack, December 7, 2016, only five survivors from the ship were still living.[8]

The USS *Arizona* Memorial is now part of the World War II Valor in the Pacific Monument, which has nine sites, three in the Aleutian Islands in Alaska, one in California, and the other five in Pearl Harbor, including the USS *Arizona* Memorial, the USS *Oklahoma* Memorial, the USS *Utah* Memorial, and parts of Ford Island and Battleship Row.

⚓ *An aerial view provides a clear perspective of how the memorial is situated as a bridge over the sunken* USS Arizona.

Chapter 8

PRESERVE AND PROTECT

The US naval base in Pearl Harbor became a National Historic Landmark in 1965. The navy continued to oversee the USS *Arizona* Memorial until 1980, when jurisdiction was moved from the navy to the National Park Service (NPS). The NPS was better equipped to preserve and protect the architectural artifacts that lay below the memorial.

Although the USS *Arizona* was a cultural treasure and one of the most famous memorials in the country, no one knew until the 1980s what was really below the white bridge memorial. All that can be seen above the surface are a few pieces of the superstructure, including the remains of a turret and the severed mainmast that flies the US flag. The rest of the ship is a murky outline below the water. Millions of people had visited the memorial, but many questions were unanswered. How much corrosion had occurred on the ship? Was there still live ammunition? Where was the oil coming from that leaked slowly but steadily to the surface?

The Submerged Cultural Resources Unit of the NPS addressed these questions. This unit promotes preservation of underwater archaeological sites such as shipwrecks. Formed in 1980, the unit began surveying the USS *Arizona* in 1983.

Diving on the Wreck

Daniel J. Lenihan, head of the team, led the first divers to explore the wreck since the 1940s. Diving conditions in the harbor are poor. The harbor is approximately 40 feet (12 m) deep with a silty bottom. The silt is constantly stirred up by harbor ship traffic and silt from the rivers that flow into the sea, making visibility poor. Divers could barely see beyond an arm's length as they swam along the corroded metal sides of the ship. As Lenihan swam, concentrating on what he was seeing before him, he looked up into the barrel of a gigantic gun. It was eerie. The intact 14-inch (36 cm) guns from turret 1 still lay below, although the navy thought they had been salvaged after the attack. Divers also discovered live 5-inch (13 cm) shells lying on the deck

An NPS diver examines the aft hatch of the USS Arizona.

directly under the memorial where thousands of visitors walked each year. The divers left the water to allow navy professionals to remove the shells.

Divers had a hard time collecting data on the shipwreck. Visibility was too poor to photograph the position of various parts of the wreck. The ship's metal was twisted and corroded, so it was impossible to use standard measuring tapes to collect information.

Diver Dave Conlin

Dave Conlin, an underwater archaeologist for the NPS, is one of the few people with access to the USS *Arizona* wreckage. He wrote about his experiences in *Scuba Diving* magazine. "The site is heavily overgrown with sponges, corals and other marine life, with a color pallet of olive and muddy brown as muted as the visitors to the memorial," recalled Conlin. "Corners and edges once polished and painted in Navy gray are rounded, bent, cut by salvage teams or shattered by blast and fire. . . . Your mood is pulled along a declining spectrum from normalcy to sadness as you see areas where fish have cleared the teak decking to lay their eggs, or a bit of new coral growth, and then suddenly a sailor's shaving kit or a cereal bowl in the galley area."[1]

Instead, divers used a method that had been developed to map archaeological sites on land. They clipped nylon line in place with clothespins every 10 feet (3 m) to create a string model over the wreck, similar to a wire-frame drawing on a computer. The points were plotted onto paper and measurements could then be taken from known points. It was long and tedious work, but eventually the team collected enough data so artists were able to create exact renderings of what the ship looked like as it lay below the harbor.

Science to the Rescue

As more information became available, more questions arose about the best way to preserve and protect the historic wreck. Scientists studied the rate of corrosion on the ship's hull using a tool called a bathycorrometer. This tool measures how electricity flows through metal. The electric readouts were later graphed in a laboratory to estimate the likelihood of corrosion at specific locations.

Another group of scientists studied what most people would call the crud that encrusts the ship. When microorganisms, algae, plants, and animals accumulate on the wreck, a process called biofouling is taking place. Biofouling protects the surface of the ship by reducing the amount of oxygen that causes corrosion from reaching the metal.

Bathycorrometers

A bathycorrometer works by touching the steel hull of a ship with an electrode that sends a small volt of electricity through the metal to measure electrical conductivity potential. This voltage is then compared with a known standard, or reference electrode, to determine the rate of corrosion. Bathycorrometers are most often used on safety inspections of bridges and deep-sea oil rigs.

Others studied the chemical composition of the water to determine both how the artifact affects the surrounding environment and how the water in the harbor may affect the ship over time. Scientists estimate that in time, polluted runoff will reduce the nutrients in the harbor water. In turn, this will damage the biofouling process that is keeping the ship's hull rigid and intact.

Black Tears

Visitors to the USS *Arizona* Memorial notice a rainbow sheen of oil on the water. Tiny drops of oil float to the surface from the submerged tanks of the ship more than 75 years after

⚓ *The NPS has undertaken a number of site studies to understand the effects of oil leaking from the wreckage.*

the sinking. Many people call these USS *Arizona*'s black tears; tears of those who still lie on the ship below.

Oil leakage was of particular concern to the scientists. Although much of the oil was burned during the inferno following the attack, estimates are that 500,000 gallons (1.9 million L) of oil remain on the ship.[2] The remaining oil floats to the surface in droplets, somewhere from two to nine quarts (2 to 8.5 L) of oil each day.[3]

If all the remaining oil were released at once, it would be an environmental disaster to the wildlife and pristine beaches of Hawaii. However, there is no easy way to solve the problem. The oil is not in just one big tank, but in bunkers spread throughout the sunken ship. This was done to protect the fuel supply in case of attack. Trying to remove the oil would require sending divers deep within the ship, now a war grave, and might make things worse as the tanks are now corroding. However, the water quality investigations showed that the interior surfaces of the ship are corroding at a lower rate than the exterior surfaces due to differences in acidity in the enclosed water of the ship and the water in the harbor. The NPS continues to monitor the problem.

More Discoveries

In 1986, divers exploring the ship noted and marked the location of every artifact on deck: silverware, bottles, a medicine chest, a shaving kit, a cereal bowl, and many more. Some items were heavily corroded or encrusted. Others, especially those with smooth, plastic surfaces, remained clean. Divers did not remove the objects, but the maps indicating their locations were

The USS Arizona in Pop Culture

The USS *Arizona* was a part of popular culture even before the events at Pearl Harbor. James Cagney and Walter O'Brien starred in the 1934 movie *Here Comes the Navy*, a comedy about two sailors that was filmed aboard the USS *Arizona*.

Since the attack, more than a dozen movies featuring Pearl Harbor have been produced, including *From Here to Eternity* (1953), *In Harm's Way* (1965), *Tora! Tora! Tora!* (1970), and *Pearl Harbor* (2001). There have also been documentaries, a TV miniseries, and dozens of books, both nonfiction and fiction, produced on the topic.

Songs about Pearl Harbor began playing immediately after the December 7 attack. Songwriters Cliff Friend and Charles Tobias wrote "We Did It Before (and We Can Do It Again)" on the day of the attack. It was on the radio three days later, sung by Eddie Cantor, reminding Americans of their role in World War I and their triumph over their adversaries. One of the most popular songs, "Remember Pearl Harbor," with music by Don Reid and Sammy Kaye and performed by Kaye, was recorded just ten days after the attack. Many of the early songs were angry and racist in nature, but these gave way to songs of patriotism, such as J. Fred Coot's "Goodbye Mama (I'm Off to Yokohama)."

Ben Affleck, left, and Josh Hartnett, center, are caught in the cross fire of the Japanese attack in the movie Pearl Harbor.

94

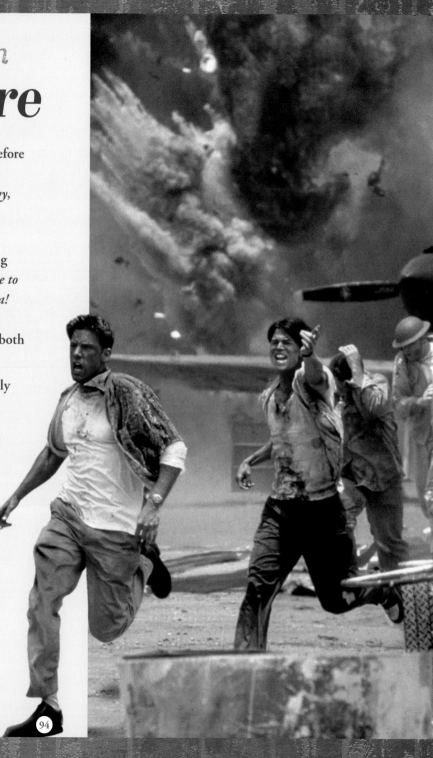

used to recreate the eight-foot (2 m) model of the ship that is now on display in the visitor's center. The dive was documented by the BBC network in a series called *Discoveries Underwater*.

With time, technology has improved, and the dive expeditions on the USS *Arizona* have uncovered more information. For the seventy-fifth anniversary of the Pearl Harbor attack in 2016, the television network PBS filmed the investigation. New remotely operated vehicles were designed to explore the interior rooms of the ship. Researchers carefully chose openings in the wreck that would not disturb the surface infrastructure or the silt layer covering the ship. Of special interest was monitoring the interior walls of the ship that contain the oil still on board.

Today, the USS *Arizona* is slowly being reclaimed by the sea. Approximately seven inches (18 cm) of silt covers most of the hull.[4] Underwater life, much of which consists of exotic species that arrive with other ships in the busy harbor, thrives in the new ecosystem created by the wreck. The USS *Arizona* is the home of many marine animals, including brown sea horses, corals, sponges, and spotted eagle rays.

The USS Arizona on the Mainland

Items from the USS *Arizona* have made their way to other memorials around the country. In 1944, Bill Bowers discovered one of the two bells salvaged from the USS *Arizona* at the Puget Sound Naval Shipyard in Washington State. The bell was about to be melted down.

Pearl Harbor Remembrance Day

On August 23, 1994, the US Congress designated December 7 as National Pearl Harbor Remembrance Day. Remembrance events are held on this day at the USS *Arizona* Memorial. Traditionally, flags displayed by Americans on their homes, at the White House, and on government buildings are flown at half-staff until sunset to honor those who died during the attack at Pearl Harbor.

Bowers acquired the bell for the University of Arizona, and it was installed in a specially built clock tower on the campus. The rescued 1,820-pound (816 kg) bell is rung seven times on the third Wednesday of each month at 12:07 p.m. in remembrance of the attack, as well as for other special occasions. The bell moved to the new student union building in 2002.[5]

On December 7, 2016, the University of Arizona dedicated a new memorial in remembrance of the USS *Arizona* that shows the gigantic shape of the ship. The memorial, on the center mall of the campus, features an outline of the ship that is 597 feet (182 m) long and 97 feet (30 m) wide.[6] Although the university had a scale model of the ship, the new memorial gives a greater sense of the size and magnitude of the loss. A small plaza marks the position of the ship's foremast, displaying inscriptions of the names of those who died.

Phoenix, the capital of Arizona, and other towns in the state also have memorials featuring parts of the ship's superstructure. An oil-stained flag that flew on one of the smaller boats stored on the USS *Arizona*'s deck, along with the captain's silverware and serving platters, can be viewed in the Arizona Capitol Museum. The ship's signal mast, an anchor, and a gun barrel are on display in Wesley Bolin Memorial Plaza on the state capitol grounds.

A New America Emerges

Pearl Harbor, and the symbol of that day, the USS *Arizona*, changed the United States and the rest of the world. It was the event that brought the United States into World War II and established the United States as a world power. Americans knew after Pearl Harbor that they could no longer ignore events happening in the rest of the world. "Remember Pearl Harbor" became more than a rallying cry for revenge on America's enemies. It became a remembrance to remain vigilant and prepared, and to honor those people who serve to protect the country.

Today, the USS *Arizona* Memorial honors all the people—naval, military, and civilian—who died in the attack. In addition, it has become a living research site for scientists to investigate, and they can later use their findings to protect other underwater archaeological sites.

Timeline

1913

⚓ The US government orders the USS *Arizona* to be built.

1914

⚓ Construction of the USS *Arizona* begins on March 16 at the Brooklyn Navy Yard.

1915

⚓ On June 19, the USS *Arizona* is christened and launched.

1916

⚓ On October 17, the ship is commissioned by the US Navy.

1917

⚓ On April 3, the ship takes its place at Norfolk Navy Base, only three days before the United States enters World War I.

1919

⚓ The USS *Arizona* is sent to the Mediterranean to support US interests during the conflict between Greece and Turkey.

1933

⚓ Crewmen of the USS *Arizona* provide aid to the victims of an earthquake in Long Beach, California.

1934

⚓ The movie *Here Comes the Navy* is filmed aboard the USS *Arizona*.

1939

⚓ The USS *Arizona* is updated with new, larger guns and antiaircraft guns.

1940

⚓ In June, President Roosevelt orders the Pacific Fleet moved from California to Pearl Harbor.

⚓ In July, Congress orders an embargo on Japan, halting the shipment of airplanes and aviation fuel.

1941

⚓ On October 22, the USS *Arizona* is damaged during an accident with the USS *Oklahoma*.

⚓ On December 7, Japan launches a surprise attack at Pearl Harbor. The attack kills 2,403 people, heavily damages the Pacific Fleet, and sinks the USS *Arizona*.

⚓ The United States declares war on Japan on December 8, officially joining the combat in World War II.

1945

⚓ In August, the United States drops atomic bombs on Hiroshima, Japan, and Nagasaki, Japan, bringing an end to World War II.

1949

⚓ A commission begins plans to build a permanent memorial at the site of the USS *Arizona*.

1962

⚓ The USS *Arizona* Memorial is officially dedicated and opens to the public.

1980

⚓ The navy relinquishes care of the USS *Arizona* Memorial to the National Park Service.

1983

⚓ The first scientific expedition to the wreck sends divers to map the remains of the ship so they can be protected and preserved.

Essential Facts

What Happened

The USS *Arizona*, a navy battleship built to defend United States territory during times of war, was hit by Japanese bomber planes. The ship carried more than 1,500 crewmen, 1,177 of whom died during the attack. More than one-half of the total naval casualties in the attack were from the USS *Arizona*.

When It Happened

The USS *Arizona* was attacked by Japanese forces and sunk on December 7, 1941, bringing the United States into World War II.

Where It Happened

The attack on the USS *Arizona* and other US battleships occurred in Pearl Harbor, a US naval base on the island of Oahu in Hawaii.

Key Players

- Franklin D. Roosevelt was president when the United States entered World War II. His calm leadership and the trust he instilled in the American public rallied the United States to get behind the war effort.

- Isoroku Yamamoto was the architect of the surprise attack on Pearl Harbor. He warned the Japanese government that if the Japanese troops could not win against the American troops in the first months of the war, the Japanese would not win at all.

- US Navy Rear Admiral Samuel Glenn Fuqua helped save 70 wounded people during the attack on Pearl Harbor. His actions later earned him the Medal of Honor.

Legacy

The sneak attack on Pearl Harbor, and especially the massive loss of life on the USS *Arizona*, galvanized the people of the United States to retaliate against Japan and enter World War II on the side of the Allies. In the months after the attack, the US Navy decided to leave the sunken USS *Arizona* at the bottom of the harbor. The unrecovered bodies of the crewmen were considered "lost at sea." In 1962, long after the war had ended, the USS *Arizona* Memorial was unveiled and opened to the public. This memorial was built over the site of the sunken ship. It reminds visitors about the courage and sacrifices of US Navy crewmen during World War II.

Quote

"Yesterday, December 7, 1941—a date that will live in infamy—the United States of America was suddenly and deliberately attacked by naval and air forces of the Empire of Japan."

—*Franklin D. Roosevelt*

Glossary

bow
The forward part of a ship; the point that is most forward when the ship is underway.

complement
All officers and enlisted people on a ship, excluding guests and visitors.

conning tower
A raised platform from which an officer can give directions to a helmsman.

displacement
The weight of the volume of water displaced by a ship, used to tell the weight of a ship.

enlist
To enroll in the armed services.

fleet
A group of ships that sails together for the same purpose and under one command.

infamy
Being well-known for a bad quality or act.

keel
A center line running along the bottom of a ship for strength, often referred to as the backbone.

liberty
Permission to leave the ship for a short amount of time, usually two days or less.

magazine
A place where ammunition or explosive materials are stored.

maneuvers
A large military exercise involving troops, warships, and other forces.

moor
To fasten a ship to an anchor by using a rope or cable.

scullery
A place where dishes are washed.

shrapnel
Small metal fragments that are flung into the air by an exploding shell or bomb, causing risk of injury or death to anyone nearby.

slipway
A space in a shipyard where there is a foundation for launching and that is occupied by a ship while under construction.

strafe
To attack from the air at close range by low-flying aircraft with machine guns or cannons.

trajectory
The path or progression of an object as it moves through space.

turret
A place from which guns are fired that provides visibility and protection.

Additional Resources

Selected Bibliography

Gillon, Steven M. *Pearl Harbor: FDR Leads the Nation into War*. New York: Perseus, 2011. Print.

Madsen, Daniel. *Resurrection: Salvaging the Battle Fleet at Pearl Harbor*. Annapolis, MD: Naval Institute, 2003. Print.

Stratton, Donald. *All the Gallant Men: The First Memoir by a USS* Arizona *Survivor*. New York: HarperCollins, 2016. Print.

Further Readings

Allen, Thomas B. *Remember Pearl Harbor: American and Japanese Survivors Tell Their Stories*. Washington, DC: National Geographic, 2015. Print.

Edwards, Sue Bradford. *The Bombing of Pearl Harbor*. Minneapolis: Abdo, 2016. Print.

Garland, Sherry. *Voices of Pearl Harbor*. Gretna, LA: Pelican, 2013. Print.

Zullo, Allan. *Heroes of Pearl Harbor: Ten True Tales*. New York: Scholastic, 2016. Print.

Online Resources

To learn more about the USS *Arizona*, visit **abdobooklinks.com**. These links are routinely monitored and updated to provide the most current information available.

More Information

For more information on this subject, contact or visit the following organizations:

National Park Service

WWII Valor in the Pacific National Monument
1845 Wasp Blvd. Bldg. 176
Honolulu, HI 96818
808-422-3399
nps.gov/valr/index.htm

The National Park Service oversees the memorial and monitors conditions on the wreck.

Sons and Daughters of Pearl Harbor Survivors

President: Deidre Kelley
PO Box 1022
Yulee, FL 32041
904-225-0013
sdphs.org

This organization is dedicated to remembering the USS *Arizona*. It publishes a newsletter, *Offspring*.

University of Arizona

Special Collections at the University of Arizona Libraries
1510 E. University Blvd.
Tucson, AZ 85721
speccoll.library.arizona.edu/online-exhibits

The University of Arizona has a memorial on the mall contained within a life-size silhouette of the USS *Arizona*. The University Libraries Special Collections contain artifacts and photographs from the ship.

Source Notes

Chapter 1. A Day of Infamy

1. Donald Stratton. *All the Gallant Men: An American Sailor's Firsthand Account of Pearl Harbor.* New York: HarperCollins, 2016. Print. 67.

2. Ibid.

3. Ibid. 78–83.

4. Gary Hicks. "Awakening the Sleeping Giant: The Birth of the Greatest Generation." *US Department of Veterans Affairs.* US Department of Veterans Affairs, 6 Dec. 2013. Web. 15 Sept. 2017.

5. "Remembering Pearl Harbor." *National Geographic.* National Geographic, 2001. Web. 7 June 2017.

6. Donald Stratton. *All the Gallant Men: An American Sailor's Firsthand Account of Pearl Harbor.* New York: HarperCollins, 2016. Print. 64.

7. Ibid.

8. "The Japanese Attacked Pearl Harbor December 7, 1941." *America's Story from America's Library.* Library of Congress, n.d. Web. 15 Sept. 2017.

9. Steven M. Gillon. *Pearl Harbor: FDR Leads the Nation into War.* New York: Basic, 2011. Print. 48.

10. Donald Stratton. *All the Gallant Men: An American Sailor's Firsthand Account of Pearl Harbor.* New York: HarperCollins, 2016. Print. 80.

11. Steven M. Gillon. *Pearl Harbor: FDR Leads the Nation into War.* New York: Basic, 2011. Print. 48.

Chapter 2. The Dreadnoughts

1. Jordan Golson. "How WWI's U-Boats Launched the Age of Unrestricted Warfare." *Wired.* Condé Nast, 22 Sept. 2014. Web. 3 July 2017.

2. "USS *Arizona* BB-39 Statistics." *USSArizona.org.* Nancy A. Nease, 12 Nov. 1999. Web. 15 Sept. 2017.

3. Shaun McKinnon. "USS *Arizona*: Before Pearl Harbor, the Mightiest Ship at Sea." *Arizona Republic.* Arizona Republic, 5 Dec. 2014. Web. 7 June 2017.

4. Ibid.

5. "*Arizona* Afloat as 75,000 Cheer." *New York Times.* New York Times, 20 June 1915. Web. 15 Sept. 2017.

6. "Grease! 30,000 Pounds of It to Launch 'Biggest Battleship' *Arizona*; Placed on End, Taller Than 24-Story Building." *USSArizona.org*. The Wichita Beacon, 19 June 1915. Web. 15 Sept. 2017.

7. Shaun McKinnon. "USS *Arizona*: Before Pearl Harbor, the Mightiest Ship at Sea." *Arizona Republic*. Arizona Republic, 5 Dec. 2014. Web. 7 June 2017.

8. "*Arizona* II (Battleship No. 39)." *Naval History and Heritage Command*. Naval History and Heritage Command, 9 Nov. 2004. Web. 15 Sept. 2017.

Chapter 3. A Sailor's Life

1. Iain Woessner. "In Life, USS *Arizona* Had Movie Role, Scandal." *East Valley Tribune*. East Valley Tribune, 6 Dec. 2009. Web. 15 Sept. 2017.

2. John Wilkens. "75 Years Later, Keeping Pearl Harbor Memories Alive." *San Diego Union-Tribune*. San Diego Union-Tribune, 4 Dec. 2016. Web. 15 Sept. 2017.

3. Donald Stratton. *All the Gallant Men: An American Sailor's Firsthand Account of Pearl Harbor*. New York: HarperCollins, 2016. Print. 56.

4. Ibid. 51.

5. *At 'Em Arizona* 17.22 (22 Apr. 1921). *National Parks Service*. Web. 15 Sept. 2017.

Chapter 4. Peacetime Missions

1. Shaun McKinnon. "USS *Arizona*: Before Pearl Harbor, the Mightiest Ship at Sea." *Arizona Republic*. Arizona Republic, 5 Dec. 2014. Web. 7 June 2017.

2. *Life* 9.18 (28 Oct. 1940). *Google Book Search*. Web. 15 Sept. 2017.

Chapter 5. Sinking the USS *Arizona*

1. Craig Nelson. *Pearl Harbor: From Infamy to Greatness*. New York: Scribner, 2016. Print. 281.

2. Duane Vachon. "Rear Admiral Samuel Glenn Fuqua, U.S. Army, U.S. Navy: Soldier, Sailor Turned Hero." *Hawaii Reporter*. Hawaii Reporter, 25 Apr. 2011. Web. 15 Sept. 2017.

3. Collin Makamson. "'Praise the Lord and Pass the Ammunition!!'" *The National WWII Museum*. The National WWII Museum, 10 Oct. 2012. Web. 15 Sept. 2017.

Source Notes Continued

4. Shaun McKinnon. "Survivors of the Attack on USS *Arizona*: Those Who Will Gather, Those Who Will Be Laid to Rest." *Arizona Republic*. Arizona Republic, 6 Dec. 2016. Web. 15 Sept. 2017.

5. Vincent James Vlach Jr. "USS *Arizona* History." *USSArizona.org*. Nancy A. Nease, 12 Nov. 1999. Web. 15 Sept. 2017.

6. Craig Nelson. *Pearl Harbor: From Infamy to Greatness*. New York: Scribner, 2016. Print. 313.

7. "Remembering Pearl Harbor: A Pearl Harbor Fact Sheet." *United States Census Bureau*. National World War II Museum, n.d. Web. 7 June 2017.

8. George Petras. "Dec. 7, 1941." *USA Today*. USA Today, 6 Dec. 2016. Web. 15 Sept. 2017.

9. Ibid.

Chapter 6. An Angry Country
1. "1914: FDR Reacts to News of Pearl Harbor Bombing." *History.com*. A&E Networks, 2009. Web. 7 June 2017.

2. Steven M. Gillon. *Pearl Harbor: FDR Leads the Nation into War*. New York: Basic, 2011. Print. 122.

3. Franklin D. Roosevelt. "Proposed Message to the Congress." *US National Archives and Records Administration*. US National Archives and Records Administration, 7 Dec. 1941. Web. 15 Sept. 2017.

4. Frank Freidel and Hugh Sidey. "Franklin D. Roosevelt." *The White House*. The White House Historical Administration, 2006. Web. 15 Sept. 2017.

5. "Archives." *Royal Oak Historical Society*. Royal Oak Historical Society, n.d. Web. 15 Sept. 2017.

6. "American Women in World War II." *History.com*. A&E Networks, 2010. Web. 7 June 2017.

7. Stephen Daggett. "Costs of Major U.S. Wars." *Congressional Research Service*. Congressional Research Service, 29 June 2010. Web. 15 Sept. 2017.

8. Roger Pusey. "Savings Stamps Gone, But We Still Feel a 'Bond' with Treasury." *Deseret News*. Deseret Digital Media, May 15, 1988. Web. 19 Sept. 2017.

9. "Bombing of Hiroshima and Nagasaki." *History.com*. A&E Networks, 2009. Web. 15 Sept. 2017.

Chapter 7. Lest We Forget

1. US Naval Institute Staff. "How Elvis Helped Save the USS *Arizona* Memorial." *US Naval Institute News*. US Naval Institute, 7 Dec. 2016. Web. 7 June 2017.

2. Ibid.

3. "The Construction of the USS *Arizona* Memorial." *Pearl Harbor Visitor's Bureau*. Pearl Harbor Visitors Bureau, 17 Feb. 2016. Web. 18 Aug. 2017.

4. "Submerged Cultural Resources Study: USS *Arizona* and Pearl Harbor National Historic Landmark." *National Park Service*. National Park Service, 27 Apr. 2001. Web. 7 June 2017.

5. "World War II Valor in the Pacific: Frequently Asked Questions." *National Park Service*. National Park Service, 8 Sept. 2017. Web. 15 Sept. 2017.

6. "How Many Died on the USS *Utah*?" *Pearl Harbor Visitors Bureau*. Pearl Harbor Visitors Bureau, n.d. Web. 18 Aug. 2017.

7. Craig Nelson. *Pearl Harbor: From Infamy to Greatness*. New York: Scribner, 2016. Print. 415.

8. Wayne Yoshioka. "On The 75th Anniversary of Pearl Harbor, Only A Few Survivors Remain." *National Public Radio*. National Public Radio, 7 Dec. 2016. Web. 15 Sept. 2017.

Chapter 8. Preserve and Protect

1. Dave Conlin. "Diving to Preserve the USS *Arizona*, 75 Years After the Attack on Pearl Harbor." *ScubaDiving.com*. Scuba Diving Magazine, 4 Dec. 2016. Web. 17 July 2017.

2. "World War II Valor in the Pacific: Frequently Asked Questions." *National Park Service*. National Park Service, 8 Sept. 2017. Web. 15 Sept. 2017.

3. Ibid.

4. "World War II Valor in the Pacific National Monument: USS *Arizona*." *National Park Service*. National Park Service, n.d. Web. 7 June 2017.

5. "Bell from the USS *Arizona*." *University of Arizona*. University of Arizona, n.d. Web. 15 Sept. 2017.

6. "Hellas Construction Teams Up on USS *Arizona* Mall Memorial at University of Arizona." *Hellas Construction*. Hellas Construction, 7 Dec. 2016. Web. 15 Sept. 2017.

Index

About the Author

Cynthia Kennedy Henzel has a bachelor of science in social studies education and a master of science in geography. She has worked as a teacher-educator in many countries. Currently, she works writing books and developing education materials for social studies, history, science, and English-language students. She has written more than 80 books for young people, including the Abdo series Troubled Treasures.